DRAGON MASTERS

HEAT OF THE LAVA DRAGON

TRACEY WEST

SCHOLASTIC INC.

DRAGON MASTERS

Read All the Adventures

TABLE OF CONTENTS

FOR JESSIKA, DAVE, ALLORA, AND SHAWN.

Each of you has a special place in my heart. — TW

While Dragon Masters takes place in a fantasy world, many of the places and people resemble those here on Earth. The author would like to thank Dr. Bernida Webb-Binder for providing her expertise in the art and history of the Pacific Islands for this book.

The publisher does not have any control over and does not assume any responsibility for author or third-party websites or their content.

Library of Congress Cataloging-in-Publication Data

Names: West, Tracey, 1965- author. | Howells, Graham, illustrator. | West, Tracey, 1965- Dragon Masters; 18.

Title: Heat of the lava dragon / Tracey West ; illustrated by Graham Howells.

Description: First edition. | New York : Branches/Scholastic, 2021. | Series: Dragon masters ; 18 | Summary: Drake's friends Mina and Caspar, their dragons, and Worm were trapped in stone by the evil wizard Astrid who has stolen their dragons' powers, but Drake himself was saved from a similar fate by Astrid's sister Hulda; now because of his strong connection with Worm, Drake is able to help his dragon to break free, but to free the others they need the assistance of three other dragons—a lava dragon, a sea dragon, and a wind dragon—and they have to do it before Astrid can steal the powers of even more dragons.
Identifiers: LCCN 2020008914 | ISBN 9781338635454 (paperback) |
ISBN 9781338635461 (library binding) | ISBN 9781338635478 (ebook)
Subjects: LCSH: Dragons—Juvenile fiction. | Magic—Juvenile fiction. | Wizards—Juvenile fiction. | Rescues—Juvenile fiction. | Adventure stories. | CYAC: Dragons—Fiction. | Magic—Fiction. | Wizards—Fiction. Rescues—Fiction. | Adventure and adventurers—Fiction. | LCGFT: Action and adventure fiction.
Classification: LCC PZ7.W51937 Hc 2021 | DDC 813.54 [Fic]—dc23
LC record available at https://lccn.loc.gov/2020008914

10 9 8 7 6 5 4 3 2 1 21 22 23 24 25

Printed in China 62

First edition, March 2021
Illustrated by Graham Howells
Edited by Katie Carella

WORM NEEDS HELP

Drake, are you there?

Drake heard the voice of his dragon, Worm, in his head. His eyes got wide.

Just a few minutes before, Drake and Worm had been in the land of Navid, at the Fortress of the Stone Dragon. There, an evil wizard named Astrid had stolen the Stone Dragon's powers. Then she used those powers to transform Drake's friends Mina and Caspar into stone, along with their dragons.

Astrid had turned Worm into stone, too.

Astrid's sister, Hulda, rescued Drake just in time, before he could be turned to stone. She used magic to bring him to the Castle of the Wizards in Belerion. Hulda and Jayana, the Head Wizard at the castle, said they would help the others left behind.

Still, Drake worried that Worm might be stuck as a statue forever. But now . . .

"I just heard Worm's voice!" Drake cried.

"Excellent!" said Jayana.

Drake looked into the magic mirror he held in his hand. His friend Ana's face looked back at him. She just had contacted him from King Roland's castle in Bracken.

"Give me a minute," he told Ana. "I'm going to try to talk to Worm."

Then he answered his Earth Dragon.

I'm in the Castle of the Wizards, Worm, Drake replied. *Where are you? I saw you turned into stone!*

I am still in Navid, and I am still stone, Worm replied. *I think I can break free, but I need your help, Drake. Please go outside the castle! Then I will tell you what to do.*

I'm going now! Drake told Worm, and he jumped out of his chair.

"Drake, what did Worm say?" Ana asked.

"He needs my help!" Drake answered. "I have to go!"

"Good luck!" Ana called out from the mirror. Then her face vanished.

Drake rushed outside. Jayana and Hulda followed him. The castle stood on the edge of a cliff overlooking the ocean. Below, he could hear the waves crashing against the shore.

Drake took a deep breath. *I hope this works*, he thought.

A STRONG CONNECTION

Drake reached out to Worm with his mind. *Worm, can you still hear me? I'm outside now!*

I can hear you, Worm said. *Because I am an Earth Dragon, I think I can break through the powers of the Stone Dragon that have made me a statue. I just need more energy.*

Where can you get more energy? Drake asked him.

From, you, Drake! Worm replied. *We have a strong connection. Our combined energy should give me the power I need.*

What do I need to do? Drake asked.

Close your eyes, Worm said. *Concentrate on me. Imagine your energy connecting to mine.*

Drake closed his eyes. He imagined a green wave of glowing energy reaching all the way to Navid and touching the Earth Dragon.

"Drake, your Dragon Stone is glowing very brightly!" Jayana cried.

Like every Dragon Master, Drake wore a piece of the Dragon Stone around his neck. It glowed whenever he connected with Worm.

Now imagine me breaking through the stone, Worm instructed.

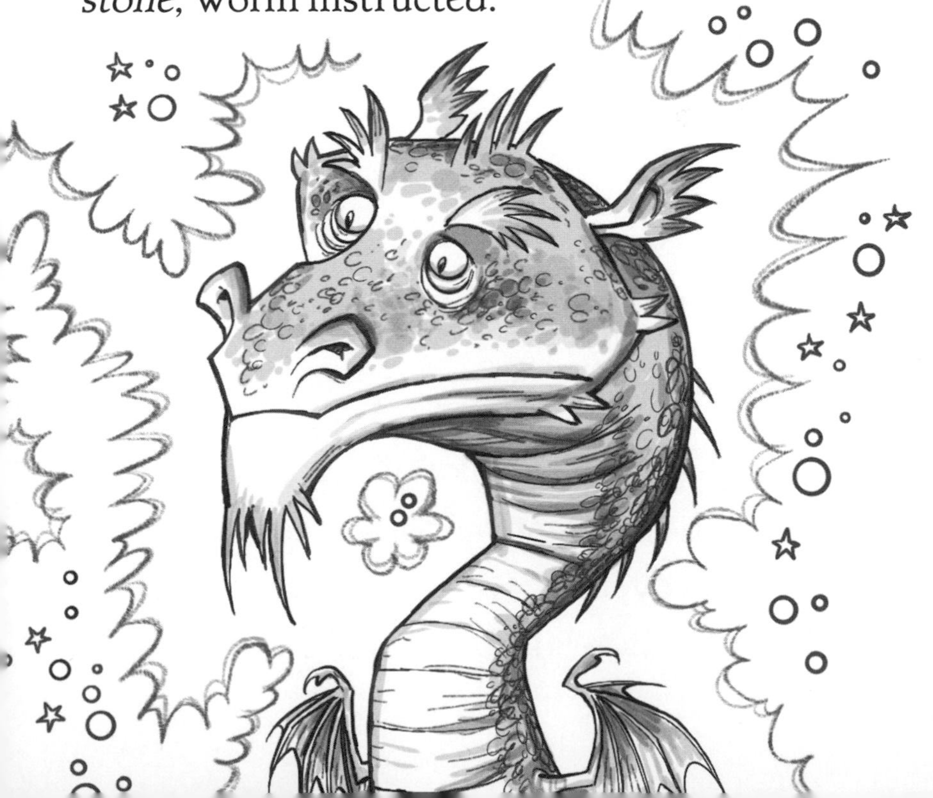

Drake pictured Worm as he'd last seen him: a big stone statue. He imagined the stone cracking. He pictured Worm breaking free. In his vision, the gray stone shattered into a million bits. The stone dust blew away. There stood Worm. Worm, with his brown scales, his kind eyes, and his big, shaggy head.

The light from Drake's Dragon Stone was so bright now that he could see it through his closed eyelids. His whole body tingled as the energy flowed through it.

Come on, Worm, he thought. *You can do it! Break free!*

The light from his Dragon Stone faded. Drake opened his eyes.

Worm wasn't there.

Drake looked at Jayana and Hulda. "I don't think it worked," he said.

Suddenly a green light flashed in front of him, and he jumped back. When the light faded, a large brown dragon sat there.

"Worm!" Drake cried.

CHAPTER 3

STOP ASTRID!

Drake threw both arms around Worm's neck.

"I've never seen such a strong connection between a Dragon Master and a dragon!" Jayana remarked.

"Yes, good work!" Hulda said.

Drake patted Worm. "Astrid told me you would be a statue forever."

Astrid was wrong, Worm said.

Hulda looked at Jayana. "Astrid has control of the fortress now. There is nobody to keep her away from the bones of the beasts."

Drake shivered as he remembered the bones inside the Fortress of the Stone Dragon. Caspar had said that they belonged to enormous beasts who once roamed the earth. Astrid wanted to use a spell to bring the bones to life: a False Life spell.

“We have to stop Astrid,” Drake said. “Her stone powers have probably worn off by now. But she has other stolen dragon powers she can use against us.”

Jayana nodded. “She is dangerous, indeed. She will not be easy to defeat.”

“The spell is complicated. It takes time to prepare the ingredients before the spell can be cast,” Hulda said. “We should have a few days to stop her.”

"What if we can't stop her from casting it?" Drake asked.

"Then we must break the spell," Jayana replied.

Drake remembered something. "Bo's Water Dragon, Shu, can break spells with her mist."

Jayana shook her head. "One dragon's mist would not be powerful enough to break the False Life spell. This is very strong magic. That is why we asked Griffith to find a way to reverse it."

"Ana told me she found a way to break the spell," Drake said. "But we need to find three dragons first."

"Then you Dragon Masters must begin the search immediately," Jayana said. "You and Worm should get back to Bracken."

"And I will return to the Land of the Far North," Hulda said. "Astrid is still angry that King Albin banished her. She has never forgiven our people for turning their backs on her. I must help them prepare for a possible attack."

Hulda snapped her fingers. *Poof!* She disappeared.

Drake turned to Jayana. "Can't we stop Astrid *before* she casts the spell?" he asked. "She is all alone in the fortress."

"Astrid is very powerful, but we can try. I will gather as many wizards as I can and go to Navid," Jayana said. "Maybe we can slow her down. And we will work to save those who were turned to stone."

“Please do all that you can,” Drake said, and then he put his hand on Worm. “To King Roland’s castle!”

THREE DRAGONS

Seconds later, Drake and Worm appeared in the Training Room in King Roland's castle.

Rori, Ana, and Bo ran out of the Dragon Masters' classroom. Drake smiled when he saw his friends.

Bo hugged Drake. "I am glad you are safe," he said.

"Thank you," Drake replied. "But Mina and Caspar and their dragons . . ."

"The wizards will help them," Rori said. "What we need to do is stop Astrid!"

Ana grabbed Drake's hand. "We have a plan. Come into the classroom."

Drake turned to Worm. "Wait here," he said, and he followed the Dragon Masters. Griffith, the wizard who trained Drake and his friends, was seated at the table. Eko, a Dragon Mage, stood beside him.

"Ah, Drake," Griffith said. "Come see what Ana has found. There is a way to reverse the False Life spell."

Ana picked up a scroll. "I found this in the library in the Dragon Temple," she said. She tapped a picture of a stone. "There is a kind of stone called a Tenebrex. It can reverse the False Life spell if you combine it with the powers of three special dragons."

She unrolled the scroll. "First, a Lava Dragon melts the stone. Then a Sea Dragon cools it. Finally, a Wind Dragon blows on the stone and transforms it into a box. The box holds the magic that can break the False Life spell."

"But where do we find these three dragons?" Drake asked. "I don't even know what *lava* is."

Griffith picked up a red book. "Lava is hot, flowing rock. A wizard named Shula wrote this book about Fire Dragons. She says that a Lava Dragon is a type of Fire Dragon," he said.

"Fire Dragons are the best!" said Rori. Her dragon, Vulcan, was a Fire Dragon.

The wizard pointed at another book. It floated over to him. The pages flipped magically and landed on a picture of a group of islands in the ocean.

"There were once Lava Dragons here, on the islands of Noa," Griffith said.

"They *once* were there?" Drake asked. "Does that mean they're not there now?"

"I am not sure, but we must start our search there," Griffith replied. "Worm and Drake must go, because the islands are far away. And leave your sword behind, Drake, so the islanders know you are friendly."

"Right," Drake said, and he removed his silver sword from his belt.

"Ana, you are good at meeting new people. I would like you and Kepri to go with Drake," Griffith said.

"I'll get Kepri!" Ana cried, running out of the classroom.

"What about me?" Rori asked.

"I need you to get us a Tenebrex Stone," Griffith said. "My wizard friend Sylvie has one. She lives in King Leon's castle in Gallia. You and Vulcan will fly there. I am counting on you to convince her to give it up."

"I won't let you down!" Rori promised.

"Bo can stay here with me and Eko," Griffith continued. "We'll try to learn more about the Sea Dragon and the Wind Dragon."

Bo picked up a book. "I am on it!" he said.

Drake looked at Griffith. "What if Ana and I don't find a Lava Dragon?" he asked.

"This is our only lead," Griffith said. "I know you will do your best, Drake."

Drake went back to the Training Room. Ana and Kepri were there. The white scales of the Sun Dragon glittered in the torchlight.

Ana put one hand on Kepri and one on Worm. "Ready, Drake!" she said.

Drake touched Worm. "Take us to the islands of Noa!"

OPELI

Worm's green light faded as they landed on an island. Drake looked around.

A girl was staring into his face, her eyes wide with fear. She wore a yellow dress with a red sash. A white flower was tucked into her wavy, black hair.

"Sorry if we scared you," Drake said. "I'm Drake. This is Ana. And these are our dragons, Worm and Kepri."

"Dragons?!" the girl asked, and she took two steps back.

"They won't hurt you," Ana said. "We're friendly. We're here because we need help."

"I-I'm Opeli," the girl said, her eyes still wide. "Where did you come from? I saw a bright light, and then . . . there you were!"

"We're from Bracken, a faraway land," Drake said. "Are we on the islands of Noa?"

"Yes. We call this island Manu," Opeli answered, not taking her eyes off of Worm and Kepri. "Are you sure that those dragons won't hurt me?"

"We're sure," Drake said, and he turned to Ana. "Is there a way to show her that our dragons are friendly?"

He looked around again, thinking. It felt much warmer here than in Bracken. The sky was so blue, and the sun was so bright!

Drake smelled salt water in the air, so he knew the ocean was close by. But he couldn't see it. They had landed in a grove of tall trees with green, feathery leaves. Small white flowers grew close to the ground, and tall orange flowers waved in the gentle breeze. A waterfall cascaded down some rocks at the foot of a hill.

"I have an idea," Ana said. "Kepri, make a rainbow!"

Kepri glided over to the waterfall. She opened her mouth and aimed a beam of sunlight at the water. The light hit the misty droplets in the air, forming a small rainbow.

Opeli smiled for the first time. "Oh, that is beautiful!" she said. "A dragon with rainbow powers must be a very nice dragon. I am not afraid now. And I am sorry, because I have not welcomed you to our island. What brings you here?"

"We are looking for a Lava Dragon," Drake said.

Opeli froze. "Why?"

"An evil wizard is casting a spell," Drake replied. "A Lava Dragon can help us stop her."

"My mother, Kalama, can tell you about Lava Dragons," Opeli said. "Follow me."

NO DRAGONS ALLOWED!

"There are so many beautiful flowers here," Ana remarked as Opeli led them to her village.

"Thank you," Opeli said. "I came out here to pick some, but I found *you* instead!"

They emerged from the grove of trees onto a sandy beach. Now Drake could see the sparkling blue-green water of the ocean. A tall cone-shaped mountain seemed to rise from the waves. White puffs of smoke poured out of the top.

"Why is smoke coming out of that mountain?" Drake asked.

"It's called a volcano," Opeli explained. "Deep inside, it is very hot. That is why we see smoke. Sometimes, when the volcano gets angry, it shoots out hot lava."

Drake gasped. "Is that where the Lava Dragons live?" he asked.

"You must talk to my mother," Opeli said. "Come, we're almost to my village."

Soon they saw a cluster of homes in the distance. As they got closer, a crowd of people moved toward them. They were talking loudly and pointing at the dragons.

"Uh oh," Opeli said. "They've seen your dragons. I might be in trouble for bringing you here."

"Should we turn around?" Ana asked.

"I will tell them you are friendly," Opeli said. "It is their duty to welcome you."

A woman stepped out from the crowd. She had the same dark hair as Opeli, and the same bright, brown eyes. Necklaces of seashells and colorful stones hung around her neck.

"Opeli! Why have you brought dragons to our village?" she asked.

"It's okay, Mother," Opeli said. "This is Drake and Ana. They came from far away. Their dragons are named Worm and Kepri. They don't want to hurt us. They need our help."

Opeli's mother frowned. "I am Kalama," she said to Drake and Ana. "I am sorry, but we cannot welcome you to this village. There are no dragons allowed here."

The villagers behind her shouted in agreement.

"We don't mean any trouble," Ana said.

"Please, help us," Drake added. "It is important."

Kalama shook her head. "No dragons. That is the rule."

"But Mother, their dragons are friendly," Opeli said. "And you have the answers Drake and Ana seek. They need to know about Lava Dragons."

Kalama raised an eyebrow. "Very well," she said. "But let us move away from the village."

Kalama and Opeli walked along the wide, sandy beach. Drake, Ana, and their dragons followed.

"Why are you two asking about Lava Dragons?" Kalama asked.

"An evil wizard is about to cast a very dangerous spell," Ana explained. "And we need a Lava Dragon to stop her."

"Then I cannot help you," Kalama said. "There were Lava Dragons here once. But they are no more!"

THE FIRST LAVA DRAGONS

Drake's heart sank. "Where are those Lava Dragons? Did they go to another island? We need to find one!"

Opeli looked at her mother. "Tell them the story."

Kalama nodded. "Long ago, there were no humans on the islands of Noa. In the sky, flew birds and bats. In the ocean, swam fish and seals. And on the land, dragons roamed."

Drake looked around at the trees and the flowers and the sandy beach. He tried to imagine dragons there.

"The dragons were made of lava from the great volcano," Kalama said, pointing to the smoking mountain in the distance. "They glowed with fiery heat. Then, when humans came to the islands, the dragons attacked. They shot lava at them. The humans could not calm them. So they fought back."

"Oh no!" Ana cried. "Did the humans . . ."

"The humans did not harm them," Kalama said. "They knew the dragons were probably just afraid. So the most powerful healers used their magic to keep the dragons safe. They made the dragons part of the land."

"What does that mean?" Drake asked. "Did they bury the dragons in the ground?"

"The dragons and the land are one," Kalama replied.

Drake still wasn't sure what she meant. But he didn't want to give up.

"Are there healers nearby? Can we ask them to bring back just one Lava Dragon?" Drake asked.

"We will keep the dragon away from your people," Ana promised.

Kalama shook her head. "No. The Lava Dragons must never return," she said. "I am sorry we cannot help you. Now please, you all must leave."

Opeli spoke up. "Please, Mother, may I take them to the papaya grove to get some fruit to eat first?" she asked. "They have come such a long way."

Kalama thought about this. "You may," she said finally. "But then they must go." She turned and walked away.

"The grove is this way," Opeli said, leading them away from the village.

"We really shouldn't spend any more time here," Drake said. "We need to get back to Bracken and figure out if Lava Dragons can be found anywhere else."

Opeli looked behind her. Her mother was far away from them now.

"I might know a way to help you," she said. "I could be wrong, but I have a feeling I am right. Will you follow me?"

"Let's go!" Drake said.

THE DRAGON ROCK

"Where are we going, Opeli?" Drake asked. He and Ana had to walk quickly to keep up with her.

She stopped and turned to face them.

"You – you might think I'm silly if I tell you," she replied. "I'd rather show you."

As they walked, the sand under their feet turned to rocky ground. A strip of land extended into the ocean. Big, jagged black rocks jutted out of the ground.

"I've never seen rocks shaped like this," Drake remarked.

"This does not look like a papaya grove," Ana said.

"It's not," Opeli said. "But there's something here you should see."

She led them down the strip of land. Then she stopped in front of one very long rock with spiky points sticking out of it.

"This rock has always looked like a dragon to me," she said. "See?"

Drake studied the rock. It did look like a dragon — a dragon as big as Worm, with spikes down its back and on the end of its long tail.

"I see it!" he cried.

"I do, too," Ana said. "There is the dragon's big head!"

Opeli smiled. "Oh, I am so glad you see it, too!" she said. "Sometimes I like to sing out loud to this dragon rock. It makes me feel happy. I like to imagine there is a Lava Dragon inside, like the ones from Mother's stories."

Ana's eyes got wide. "Is that what your mother meant when she said that the Lava Dragons became part of the land?"

Opeli frowned. "I like to think so. But Mother says I have a big imagination."

"Something tells me it's more than that," Ana said, studying the rock.

Opeli touched the tall part of the rock that looked like the dragon's spiky back. "I do *feel* something when I am here. A special connection."

Drake looked at his dragon. Sometimes Worm could sense when a dragon was nearby. In the Land of Ifri, he had connected with the Rainbow Dragon, even though she was asleep in a spider's trap!

“Worm, can you feel any dragon energy here?” he asked.

I do! Worm answered. *It is weak, but I can sense it.*

“Worm feels something, too,” Drake said. “Maybe there *is* a dragon inside this rock!”

Opeli clapped her hands. “Oh, I hope it is true! How can we know for sure?”

“Maybe Kepri’s light can show us what’s inside,” Ana said. She touched her dragon. “Kepri, aim your sunbeam at this big rock.”

Kepri flew up and opened her mouth. A beam of golden, glowing sunlight poured out. Her light hit the rock.

Deep inside, Drake saw an orange glow! Something was pulsing. *Ba-bump. Ba-bump.*

Drake gasped. “Do you see that? It’s a beating heart!”

HOT AND COLD

Opeli pressed her hand against the rock, over the heart of the dragon.

"I knew there was a Lava Dragon in here," she whispered.

"You were right, Opeli," Ana said.

Drake stared in wonder at the pulsing heart.

Then he turned to Opeli. "We need to find the healers your mom talked about. We have to ask them to bring this dragon back to life!"

Opeli shook her head. "We have healers in our village, but they will not help us. They believe that Lava Dragons are too dangerous to live side-by-side with humans."

Then Drake heard Worm's voice in his head.

I am making a connection now, Worm said. *The Lava Dragon . . . he is showing me what happened. Close your eyes, Drake . . .*

Pictures popped into Drake's head. Three people in red robes stood in front of a dragon on the water's edge. The dragon had deep orange scales and his body seemed to be glowing from inside. His eyes burned yellow.

The healers raised their arms. A great wave rose up from the ocean, and the water sparkled with magical silver light. It washed over the dragon. Drake could hear the dragon roar in his head.

The wave knocked the dragon to the ground. The dragon's orange glow began to fade. His body slowly turned black and became still.

"The healers put a spell on the water," Drake said out loud. "The Lava Dragon was glowing, but when the wave hit, he turned into this rock."

The Lava Dragon says heat will help him break the healers' spell, Worm said. *But he doesn't have enough heat on his own.*

"The Lava Dragon needs heat to break the spell," Drake announced.

"Stand back, everybody, and shade your eyes," Ana said. "Kepri, blast that rock with your sunlight!"

Drake shaded his eyes as a wide band of bright sunlight streamed from Kepri's mouth. The orange glow of the dragon's heart began to spread down to the dragon's tail, and up to the dragon's head.

Orange scales rippled across the dragon's body. His front legs rose up from the ground, and his long neck stretched up toward the sky.

"The Lava Dragon is alive!" Drake cried.

ATTACK THE DRAGONS!

A hot, bubbling liquid poured through the Lava Dragon's body. His scales rippled and glowed.

"Good job, Kepri," Ana said, patting her dragon.

His name is Ka, Worm told Drake.

"He's called Ka," Drake announced.

Opeli slowly walked up to the Lava Dragon.

"Ka, it is me, Opeli," she said. "Do you know me?"

Ka looked down at Opeli and blinked. Then he let out a thundering roar.

Drake, Ana, and Opeli took a step back.

"That sounds like a happy roar," Ana remarked. "Not an angry one."

"Opeli, I think you might be Ka's Dragon Master!" Drake said. "Just like I am Worm's, and Ana is Kepri's."

"What is a Dragon Master?" Opeli asked.

"A Dragon Master is someone who makes a special connection with a dragon," Drake replied. "Usually, the Dragon Stone chooses a Dragon Master for every dragon. After you get chosen, you wear a piece of the Dragon Stone around your neck, like this one."

He held out the green stone that dangled from a gold chain around his neck.

Ana chimed in. "The stone helps the two of you communicate. That's how we can hear our dragons' voices inside our heads."

Opeli touched Ana's stone. "*This* is a Dragon Stone? But I thought it was . . ."

"ATTACK THE DRAGONS!"

A loud, angry cry filled the air. A group of villagers ran toward them. Some carried axes. Others carried clubs or spears.

Drake gasped. "Oh no!"

"Drake, we should transport to Bracken right now," Ana said, her voice rising. "Maybe Griffith can give Opeli a Dragon Stone."

"Good idea," Drake said. "Opeli, I need you to touch Ka, and then —"

"RAAAAWWWWWWWWWWWR!" Ka let out another roar — an angry one this time. He reared back on his hind legs.

Then he spewed hot lava at the attacking villagers!

THE AHI STONE

The villagers jumped out of the way as the lava hit the ground, sizzling.

The Lava Dragon reared his head back for another attack.

"Worm, freeze Ka!" Drake called out.

Worm closed his eyes. A moment later, he and Ka began to glow green. Ka stopped moving, his open mouth frozen mid-roar.

But the villagers did not slow down. One of them sent a spear flying toward Kepri. It almost hit Opeli! She dove to the side, knocking down the spear with her hand.

Then Kalama's voice rang out. "Drop your weapons! You could hurt the children!"

Someone yelled. "But the dragons –"

"I will handle this," Kalama interrupted. "Go back to the village!"

The villagers lowered their weapons and walked away.

Kalama marched toward the Dragon Masters. "Why isn't this dragon moving?" she asked.

"Worm is using the powers of his mind to freeze him," Drake answered. "He can't hurt anyone right now."

Kalama turned to her daughter. "Opeli, where did this Lava Dragon come from?" she asked.

"Mother, I wasn't imagining things when I told you about the dragon rock!" Opeli said. "It really *was* a Lava Dragon! His name is Ka!"

"He is very dangerous, Opeli," Kalama said. "The healers must send Ka back to the land."

"No, Mother, please," Opeli pleaded. "Drake and Ana think that I could be Ka's Dragon Master. That I can connect with Ka."

"She will be able to keep him calm," Ana added. "We just need to bring them back to our kingdom. Opeli needs a Dragon Stone, like this one." She touched her Dragon Stone.

"Drake, Ana, that is what I was about to tell you before we were attacked," Opeli said. "My mother wears a stone like your Dragon Stone. It is called an Ahi Stone. They come from the heart of a volcano."

Kalama looked down at her necklaces. She took off a green stone that hung from a cord. It was bigger than Drake's and Ana's Dragon Stones, and a different shape. But it glittered just like theirs.

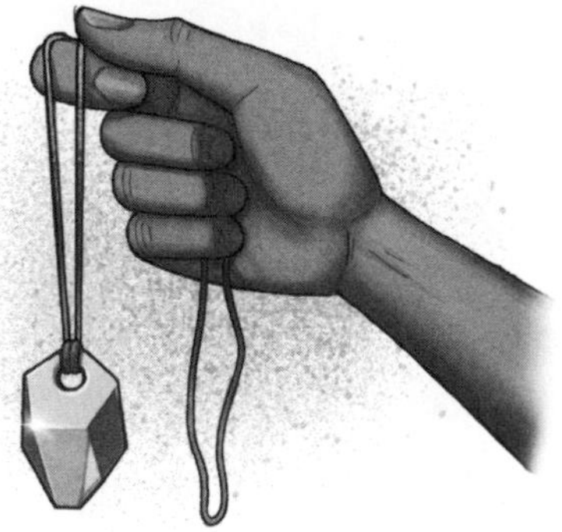

"Wow, that *does* look like a Dragon Stone!" Drake said.

"But I thought all Dragon Stones had to come from the Prime Stone," Ana said.

"Maybe the Prime Stone came from a volcano, too. We don't know for sure," Drake replied. "I think Opeli should try wearing the Ahi Stone and see if it works like a Dragon Stone."

Kalama put the stone around Opeli's neck.

Opeli turned to Drake and Ana. "Now what do I do?" she asked.

"It usually takes a long time for a dragon and a Dragon Master to connect," Drake said.

"But Ka seems to already know you, Opeli," Ana said. "Maybe you could sing to Ka like you used to sing to the dragon rock."

"It's just a silly song I made up," she said. "But I will do it."

"And to make sure no one gets hurt, Worm can keep Ka frozen until you have made a connection," Drake said. "We'll know if it works if your Dragon Stone—I mean, your Ahi Stone begins to glow."

Opeli took a deep breath and began to sing.

ANGRY AND AFRAID

Opeli sang to the Lava Dragon in a high, clear voice.

The flowers bloom in the sunlight.
The clouds drift across the blue sky.
I sit and watch the ocean waves.
As the birds go flying by by by . . .
As the birds go flying by.

"That is a beautiful song," Ana said.

"Thank you," Opeli said. Then she looked down at the Ahi Stone and frowned. "It's not glowing."

"Try another verse," Drake said.

Opeli continued to sing.

The flowers close in the moonlight.

The stars twinkle in the dark sky.

I sit and watch the ocean waves.

As the bats go flying by by by . . .

As the bats go flying by.

Drake watched Opeli's Ahi Stone. This time, as she sang, it started to faintly glow!

"Opeli, it's working!" he said. "Keep singing."

Opeli kept singing, and the Ahi Stone grew brighter.

"You're connecting!" Ana cried.

“Opeli, I am going to ask Worm to unfreeze Ka,” Drake said. “You must tell him not to attack.”

Opeli nodded. She stopped singing.

“Worm, release Ka!” Drake called out.

The green glow faded from the dragons’ bodies, and Ka began to move.

“He is angry and afraid,” Opeli said. “I can feel it.”

“Tell him that we won’t hurt him,” Ana instructed.

“Ka, stay calm,” Opeli told the Lava Dragon. “Nobody will hurt you. This is my mother, Kalama. And my friends Drake and Ana.”

Ka stopped roaring. He looked at Opeli. Her stone pulsed with green light, and her face lit up.

"I can hear Ka's words in my head!" she cried. "He says he is afraid the healers will send him back to the land. He did not like that. He was lonely, until I began to visit him."

Opeli patted the dragon's leg. "You will never be lonely again, Ka. I will stick with you," she said. "I am your Dragon Master!"

A happy sound came from the back of Ka's throat.

"I see that you have connected with this dragon, Opeli," Kalama said. "But I am not sure what we will do now. This dragon cannot stay on the island."

Drake looked at Kalama. "Can Opeli and Ka come with us for a few days?" he asked. "We still need Ka's help. And Ka needs his Dragon Master."

Kalama shook her head. "I do not know anything about where you are from, except that it is far away," she said. "Take the dragon, but I cannot let Opeli go with you!"

CHAPTER 13

KA'S PROMISE

Opeli walked up to her mother. "Being a Dragon Master is a special thing, Mother. You have always taught me to help others. Now is my chance to help the whole world."

Kalama frowned, thinking.

Drake spoke up. "I have a mother, too. I miss her, but she understands I have to travel far away so I can help others," he said. "She's very proud that I am a Dragon Master."

"And my father is very proud of me," Ana added.

Kalama sighed. "First, tell me more about the evil wizard you are fighting. Why do you need my daughter and the Lava Dragon?"

Drake and Ana explained about Astrid and her evil plan.

Kalama turned to her daughter. "I will let you go," she said. "But you must promise me that you will come home as soon as your mission is done."

“And what about Ka?” Opeli asked. “Will he be welcomed back, too?”

“I will talk to the villagers,” Kalama replied. “When our people first came to the islands, we didn’t know how to communicate with the Lava Dragons. I will tell them that you can keep Ka calm.”

Opeli nodded.

“And you must promise me not to awaken any of the other Lava Dragons who were sent back to the land,” Kalama said. “One is enough for now.”

Opeli hugged her mother. “I’m a little bit scared to leave you,” she admitted, and tears glistened in her eyes. “I will miss you.”

“I will miss you, too,” her mother replied.

Then she walked up to Ka.

“Take care of my daughter,” she told the dragon. “Keep her safe.”

Ka turned to Kalama and bowed his head.

Opeli’s Ahi Stone glowed. “Ka says that he will,” she said. “He says it is a promise he will not break.”

A NEW DRAGON MASTER

"How will you get to this faraway land?" Kalama asked Ana and Drake.

"Worm can bring us there in an instant, using his Earth Dragon powers," Drake explained. "Opeli, in order to transport, you need to touch Worm with one hand, and Ka with the other."

Opeli obeyed, and Ana did the same with Kepri.

"Good-bye, Mother!" Opeli called out. She looked around at the island. "Good-bye, Manu. I'll be back!"

Drake looked at Opeli. "This experience might make your stomach flip. But it doesn't hurt."

She took a deep breath. “I’m ready.”

“Worm, transport us all to the Training Room!” Drake cried.

Green light flashed as they disappeared from the island.

Seconds later, they appeared back in King Roland's castle.

Bo and Rori ran up to them, followed by Griffith and Eko.

"Drake! You found the Lava Dragon!" Bo cried. "And a new friend!"

"Yes, this is Ka, and his Dragon Master, Opeli," Drake said.

"It is nice to meet you all," Opeli said. She looked around the underground room, wide-eyed. "This is a very big place."

"Welcome, Opeli," Griffith said. "And well done, Drake and Ana."

"Vulcan and I did a good job, too," Rori chimed in. "We got the Tenebrex Stone from Gallia."

"That's great!" Drake said. "Now we just need a Sea Dragon and a Wind Dragon."

Griffith walked around Ka, his blue eyes sparkling with excitement. "What a beautiful dragon you are, Ka! I have been studying the connection between Fire Dragons and Lava Dragons. I'd love to see both dragons in action."

Bo stared at the lava pulsing under Ka's scales. "Rori, I think Ka looks even hotter than Vulcan," he said.

Rori folded her arms. "I don't think so. Let's bring them out into the Valley of Clouds right now and test it out!"

"I would love to, Rori, but there is so much to do," Griffith said. Then he looked at Opeli. "That is a very interesting green stone you are wearing."

"Thank you. It is an Ahi Stone," Opeli answered. "But it works just like a Dragon Stone. It glows whenever Ka and I make a connection."

Griffith stroked his long beard. "Very interesting. I should like to study your stone someday."

"We need to find the Sea Dragon next," Ana said. "Do you know where we can find one?"

Bo nodded. "Yes, we found a book that says we need to go to —"

Poof! A wizard appeared in a cloud of glittering dust.

NEWS FROM NAVID

"Jayana!" Griffith cried. "What are you doing here?"

The glittering dust disappeared. The Head Wizard's eyes were wide with alarm.

"I came to see if you have found a way to reverse the False Life spell yet," she said.

"Not yet, I'm afraid," Griffith replied. "We have a Tenebrex Stone. But we only have one of the three dragons we need."

"Oh, that is not the news I was hoping for," Jayana said. "Astrid has been working very quickly. Now she has all of the ingredients she needs."

"Can't you just get a bunch of wizards together and attack her?" Rori asked.

"Several of us went to the Land of Navid," Jayana replied. "But Astrid's magic is stronger than I even imagined. She has placed many defense spells on the fortress to keep wizards out. We couldn't break through. But we are still trying."

"What about dragons?" Eko asked. "Will her spells keep dragons out?"

"We are not sure," Jayana replied. "Dragons might be able to get through."

Griffith spoke up. "But now that we know Astrid can steal the powers of dragons and use them as her own, it is too dangerous. Our best hope is the counterspell."

Jayana frowned. "But if you still have two more dragons to find . . ."

"Then all may be lost," Griffith said.

"What about Mina and Caspar?" Drake asked. "Have the wizards been able to free them?"

Jayana shook her head. "Not yet. We haven't been able to get close enough."

Drake clenched his fists. *This isn't right,* he thought. *Astrid is going to cast the False Life spell. Mina and Caspar and their dragons will stay stone statues forever. There has to be* something *we can do!*

And there *was* something they could do. Jayana had just said that dragons might be able to get inside the fortress. But Griffith thought that was too dangerous because Astrid might steal the dragons' powers.

Normally, Drake listened to Griffith. But not this time.

Worm escaped from Astrid once . . . Drake thought. *If I ask Griffith to let me go, he won't let me. But I have to try. There is only one thing to do.*

Drake touched Worm's neck.

"Worm, take us inside the Fortress of the Stone Dragon!" he cried.

TRACEY WEST has been thinking about creating a story about a Lava Dragon since she began writing Dragon Masters. The Astrid storyline seemed like just the right time to bring in Ka and Opeli. She hopes that readers will enjoy meeting them!

Tracey lives in the misty mountains of New York State with family, dogs, and chickens. There, it is easy to imagine dragons roaming free in the green hills.

GRAHAM HOWELLS lives with his wife and two sons in west Wales, a place full of castles and legends of wizards and dragons.

There are many stories about the dragons of Wales. One story tells of a large, legless dragon – sort of like Worm! Graham's home is also near where Merlin the great wizard is said to lie asleep in a crystal cave.

Graham has illustrated several books. He has created artwork for film, television, and board games, too. Graham also writes stories for children. In 2009, he won the Tir Na N'Og award for *Merlin's Magical Creatures*.

DRAGON MASTERS
HEAT OF THE LAVA DRAGON

Questions and Activities

Worm is able to break through the powers of the Stone Dragon. How does he do this? Reread pages 6-7.

What three dragons do the Dragon Masters need to find in order to break Astrid's False Life spell?

On page 29, Ana asks Kepri the Sun Dragon to make a rainbow. Why does Ana ask her dragon to do this?

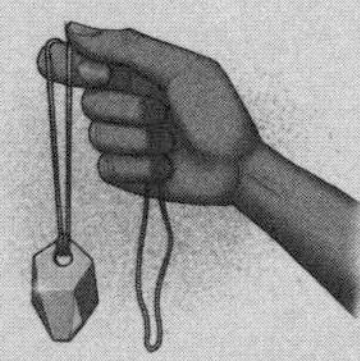

Opeli's Ahi Stone is based on a real-world stone called peridot. Peridot is a green stone that looks like a Dragon Stone. It comes from interesting places around the world! Research peridot and find out how it is formed and where it is found.

While Drake and Ana travel to Manu, Rori has her own mission to complete. Where does Rori travel to? Who does she meet there? What does she find? Write and draw Rori's adventure story!

scholastic.com/branches